ECHOES FROM HALF-QUARTER HILL

E.G. FAHIE

Copyright © 2024 Ebony G. Fahie

All rights reserved

The characters and events portrayed in this book are fictitious. Any similarity to real persons, living or dead, is coincidental and not intended by the author.

No part of this book may be reproduced, or stored in a retrieval system, or transmitted in any form or by any means, electronic, mechanical, photocopying, recording, or otherwise, without express written permission of the publisher.

ISBN-13: 9798989534128

Cover design by: Art Painter

Library of Congress Control Number: 1-13413225601
Printed in the United States of America

*To my family and friends. May your past be honored
by love, your present be celebrated with love,
and your future be full of endless love.*

CHAPTER ONE

Ladders, scaffolds, and drop cloths yet again replaced the dreamt visions of a rainbow array of tulips seen during last year's workation trip to Holland. The chaotic symphony of screeches and the buzzing of power saws filled the granular air. The sound of hammers and nail guns that greeted her every morning for the past 7 months, only reaffirmed that living amongst construction was not the best idea to date. Although she longed for the peaceful days of silent slumber and the indulgence of the modern amenities of her former residence, she knew that the push to complete the renovations to her new home was a priority. A six-month project has now lasted over 2-years.

Renee stood before the soft illuminated trimmed bathroom mirror for a final check before presenting to the army of laborers scurrying around downstairs. She traced what she initially thought was lent or carpet fibers in her hair only to discover that the unwelcome invader was anchored to her scalp. Surely, this isn't possible at 35 years young, she thought in almost a panic state. She closed her eyes, inhaled as much volume as her lungs could withstand and held her breath for a count of 10. Blowing slowly through pursed lips, she opened her eyes halfway through her daily respiratory ritual. She repeated the process two more times, then grabbed the gray hair between her finger and thumb and snatched it out. She rebuked every indication that she could imagine associated with its discovery. This is how she intended to tackle any obstacle of the day.

Renee slowly descended the grand staircase methodically, like a young lady approaching her High School prom date. She bypassed multiple trip hazards en route to the kitchen; the place that served as the tactical headquarters where most of the design decisions and plans were made. With her unconventional flare, Renee was familiar with the saying that the kitchen is the heart of the home, but in her abode, it had two. The main kitchen was adjacent to the Chef's kitchen and was also one of the few completed rooms on this week's checklist, other than 2 of the 5 guest rooms, all with ensuite bathrooms. For the most part, things were now on budget and on schedule.

Her favorite room by far was the newly converted owner's suite that she occupied during renovations. The grand bedroom suite had become her primary sanctuary. It was private and chic by her standards and perspective. She loved the large commissioned artwork that disguised the door leading to her connected home office. No expense was spared with the state of the art equipment and technology that linked to her equally impressive business office. She didn't think that it was anything less expected of what the woman titled, Tech Princess would have.

Even against the recommendation of her interior designer and college sorority sister, Tae, she was thoroughly satisfied with all of her design choices to match her minimalistic, cutting edge, and future forward taste. Renee, however relied on her designer's expertise to cohesively incorporate her husband's design taste and his favorite contemporary Italian pieces with a few of the original elements of the home that would welcome pleasant memories of his mother.

Although, it took some convincing for Renee to agree to move from her luxury high-rise condominium into the Manor, she knew that it made good business sense. She understood and desired along with Phillip, that his inherited legacy should remain in his family and be passed down appropriately as generational wealth. She simply required that the evils of the past remain behind and the goodness be brought forward physically into the present. Renee needed Mathews Manor to be a true representation of the current owners.

"Well, if it isn't the world renown interior decorator, Octavia Ross of Octavia Ross Designs, NYC."

"That is Interior Designer, not decorator darling."

"Excuse me, I stand corrected. World renowned interior designer."

"Don't worry love, you will see that costly mistake on your bill."

"Oh, I'm sure I will."

"Oh, you will."

They both switch from serious face to crazy face and have a laugh. Tae hands Renee her favorite cup with a tea bag tag hanging over the brim.

"Thanks Tae. I know that I say this every day, but I hope that you know how much I really appreciate you being here and overseeing the renovation personally."

"I know sweetie. You are my girl. Of course, I wouldn't entrust this job to anyone else. But on the other hand, you wouldn't listen to their ideas. You barely listen to mine."

"Not true. I listen. I just…"

"You just what? Girl, this place is a designer's dream. I would seriously jump at the opportunity to renovate and preserve the history and character of one of Boston's prestige mid-century homes if the right client with the right budget came along. But I do get it sis. And I fully accepted the challenge with no regrets to meld your modern aesthetics with the style of this magnificent home."

"I think that I may have bitten off more than I can chew. What made me think that I could take on a rehaul of Mathews Manor?"

"Well, you have a friend and soror who is at the top of the interior design game, who came running with enough sage to cleanse the city. Not to mention a fabulous team of talent that will land this home's reno on the front of every home inspiration magazine. I have gotten calls from a few networks wanting to feature the remaining renovation and the reveal. You should really consider it. Some of the offers are significantly substantial. It would be a win-win for both of us. I mean Renee, darling, if only these walls could talk," Tae says, full of awe and possibilities.

"I would tell the walls to shut the hell up," Renee replies jokingly,

"Well friend, the floors of this house are talking. My contractor found this beautiful tin box in one of the bedrooms under a loose floorboard while refinishing and repairing the floors. It is vintage with an elaborate lithograph design, and I would love to use it in the design. I wiped the outside, but I didn't take a look at its content. Here you go."

Tae picked up the box that sat on the granite countertop and wiped off any residual dust particles with a white cotton cloth before handing it to her client. Renee took the ornate tin box, noted it not to be too heavy. She shook it lightly near her ear to imagine its contents. Her cell phone rang, and she recognized the ring tone to be her assistant, Sasha Robinson. Although Renee believed that Sasha was more than capable of managing things at the office of her successful tech company, it was understood that her recent remote micromanaging style did not reflect a lack of confidence in her team. She placed the box on the table and headed outside to the terrace to answer the call where she could cancel out the construction noise.

By the time the last of the crew had knocked off for the day, Octavia had already ordered dinner for two to be delivered to the Manor before she realized that she had a dinner date back at the hotel restaurant with a tall, dark, and handsome airline pilot.

Usually, Renee loved the nights when Tae would sleep over and stay in one of the finished guest rooms, but tonight she welcomed more the thoughts of winding down in a warm bubble bath, then relaxing in a pair of silk pajamas, reading a good romance novel. Granted, she thought that no novel would be half as exciting as the real life stories of her friend's globe trotting love life, but tonight she desperately wanted to sleep well with hopes of good dreams.

Almost predictable, Renee traded the romance novel in for her laptop. She logged on to look at the new company website design options for RAB Inc, answered her emails, and read a few financial reports. She ultimately went down a corporate rabbit hole that made her unaware of the time. It was a text from Denise saying "Good Night" that alerted her that it was 10:30 pm. Renee texted her back, "Nite-Nite" just to acknowledge her bestie and reciprocate their exchange of affection, but surprisingly, she did not feel night-time sleepy. She decided to go downstairs to the kitchen for a cup of tea and was pleased by the installation of the new interior motion sensor lights that illuminated her path, and even more delighted that there were no electrical cords or machinery around that were visible.

Renee dispensed hot water from the coffee maker into a ceramic mug with a chamomile tea bag, then sat at the kitchen table. As the tea steeped, she grabbed a chocolate chip cookie from the glass jar on the table and took a bite.

The tin box that Octavia had given her earlier today, caught her eye. She examined and admired the ornate painted design more in depth than before. Intrigued, she removed the lid and found inside bundles of what appeared to be handwritten letters of some sort, bound by faded crimson red ribbons. She pulled out the stack on top and noticed a piece of jewelry; a silver cameo necklace with an ivory side-face silhouette of a woman on a soft pink background. She turned her attention back to the bundle, then tugged at the tail of the ribbon's bow to release the papers from the clutches of time. Renee began to read them.

If you are reading this letter or the sum of its numerous companions removed from their crypt beneath the floorboards of this wicked place, then undoubtedly, I too have met my timely demise and probably at the hands of the devil himself...or perhaps his equally as evil spawn, because I bear witness that lightning surely not only strikes the same place twice, but in my lifetime, has done so in triplicate.

As my remains surely rest upon the hill, marked where the earth and water mix, and nothing living grows, I join a sisterhood as the Seventh mistress of the manor awaiting the next who falls prey to generations of the powerful who relish inflicting a reign of terror, misfortune, and despair.

I hope that my body satisfies the hunger of the earth beneath you and that it tilts the balance of Spring. I humbly pray this is not your fate, and that I am the last.

Renee refolded the letter and placed it against her chest. She rubbed her tight belly to soothingly calm the intense kick of her baby.

CHAPTER TWO

Renee took a well deserved break after a long day of video meetings and reviewing no less than 2-dozen color swatches to reupholster her mother's wing back chairs. She shook her head just thinking about the assistant designer's presentation that revealed there were 22 similar shades between oyster shell and taupe. She decided not to make it known that her selection was made utilizing the unorthodox, yet effective method of *eeny, meeny, miny, moe* just to conclude the design session for the day. Renee thought that the chairs would make a great addition to the once dark and stuffy library. She wanted to somehow bring in some of the added historical flare and charm that Octavia always eluded to. She also wanted to include something in the decor of the room related to her warm childhood memories of her mother that would symbolically welcome her into the room of books.

Deciding to revisit the past by way of reading the memoirs of the lady who kept a tin box beneath the floor boards of her new home, Renee seized her relaxation time sprawled in comfort on the new sectional sofa, under a soothingly soft cashmere blanket, while sipping a blend of chamomile and lavender tea. Her eyes gazed upon the pages of handwritten words that would transport her 30 years before her birth.

If there was a moment that one's essence of innocence vanishes into the atmosphere to join the cloud of shame that hovers over their life; mine occurred many years ago within the walls of the Manor.

I was both happy and frightened to meet my benefactor who paved safe passage from East London's gray chambers for forgotten children, to the rich estate as Au Pair to an American child.

The downpour of rain from the night skies obscured my view from the rear and side windows of the automobile driven by the silent chauffeur. I mentally questioned his visibility as the wiper blades were indeed no match for this late winter Massachusetts night shower.

Although this was only the second time that I had ridden in a car, fatigue overtook excitement as I drifted into a deep slumber from the lullaby duet of raindrops and engine hum. My last conscious thought was that I was traveling through the haunted forest, an imaginary place in a story that I remembered being told of as a lass in the orphanage that I called home for 18 years. The car appeared to be navigated by a century of enormous trunks and naked tree branches those casted ghostly clawed shadows from the diffused light of the headlights. My comfort was in knowing that in all storytales, on the other side of a wicked forest lies a happy ever after land.

Awakened by a draft of wind from the open door, I opened my eyes to see a black pair of men's trousers from waist to calf, covered by a dark but lighter shade overcoat that kept flapping open with the wind. The contrast of his dark clothing and the scarlet red satin ribbon that disappeared into his watch pocket preempted my full focus, as I wiped moisture from my eyes. I could still hear the raindrops on the roof of the car. I poked my head out of the door opening and saw the full view of Ethan Lee, the chauffeur, who stood as emotionless as the Buckingham Guard. He was holding an open, black umbrella awaiting my exit, without verbal directions.

I stepped out on the wet cobblestone pavement with patches of lingering snow slush here and there. Covered from the rain, I adjusted my hat and tugged downward the skirting of my overcoat before deeply inhaling the moist New England air. Catching a glimpse of my worn leather suitcase sitting on the outdoor stair landing near the door to the home of my employer made me wonder how long Ethan Lee was standing outside of his vehicle waiting for me, or how long he would have waited for that matter.

I wondered if the driver was even capable of speaking. After all, an hour ago, he merely stood by this shiny black car at the depot with the rear passenger door open, holding a sign displaying my full Christian name, Elizabeth Betterton, not orphaned Beth. I, now Elizabeth, responded in the absence of cues and without question, which is important to have mastered in the household service trade.

The exterior of Mathews Manor was quite stately and modern. It's nature of appearance suggested "keep out" more so than "welcome" in the rainy night light. I caught a quick glimpse of a figure through curtain sheers in an upstairs window that darkened seconds after looking up.

I assumed that the welcoming committee was fast asleep, so I quietly followed Ethan up 3 flights of beautifully shellacked wood stairs with ornate carved handrails to the door of a bedroom at the end of the carpeted corridor. There was a dull yellow glow from the keyhole and under the door.

Ethan Lee opened the door allowing the light to escape into the dark hallway and placed my suitcase in the entryway, then he descended back down the stairs.

The first thing that I noticed was that there was only one bed in the bedroom. In my opinion, the bed could sleep at least 3 to 4 average-sized adults comfortably, nevertheless, a single bed implied that my assigned quarters would be a bedroom not shared. It would take more than a moment to fathom that this would be an actual bedroom that would be my very own.

Secondly, I was engulfed in a meadow of flowers on all 4 walls. The drapery, bedding on the bed, and wall covering were of the same floral pattern. I could not help myself from touching and even give the walls a sniff or two. But to my surprise it was as scentless and underwhelming as a conversation with Mister Ethan Lee. I assume that this is the type of decor reserved for aristocrats or royalty. I had not imagined this to be a typical American home, but I have never been to America or knew of anyone who had. The children who slept in the ward with me could barely dream of the likeness of an average traditional home in England until we became of age to deliver tendered laundry with the headmistress or carpentry items with the headmaster who bartered the crafting skills of their wards to keep the orphanage doors open. Before the war, it was rumored that the occasional secretive padding of pockets was an exchange of questionable favors.

While many of the children that I cared for were practically given away to window shoppers, some older children chose to fend for themselves without opposition. Charity became less, as families of fallen soldiers were rebuilding.

Even though I had very little belongings, I reserved unpacking until morning. I preferred to wait for specific instructions, presuming nothing at all. I was in a strange land after losing a job and the only place that I have ever called home. It was vital that I made the best impression possible for I had nowhere to go and no one to return to. For tonight, America had welcomed England's rubbage, and I deemed myself Elizabeth Betterton, Queen of Springtime.

CHAPTER THREE

The only thing better in her opinion than dinner at Monsieur Monzell's was Brunch at Monsieur Monzell's. It had been a while since Renee had left the Manor unsupervised and under the watchful eyes of a caring friend. She looked forward to catching up with all her girlfriends at once. She was excited about sharing some special news with them.

After handing her keys to the Valet, Renee was greeted with a big endearing hug from Jeffrey, the Maître D. She exchanged a few pleasantries with her Godfather about coming to the house once renovations were completed. Renee enjoyed seeing him just as much as she enjoyed dining at the restaurant. Jeffrey informed her that all of her friends had arrived and were seated. He insisted that he escort her to the table.

Renee could hear their crescendo of laughter across the room. It brought back a flood of fond memories and excitement with each step closer to the rendezvous point. She covertly hid behind Jeffrey in her approach. Laughter abruptly turned into a welcome of cheers when she peeked her head out from behind him wearing a super-sized grin. Imani, Octavia, and Denise stood up from their seats to shower her with hugs and sisterly affection.

"It is so wonderful to see all of my girls here together again at the same time."

"Long overdue Uncle J if you ask me," replied Imani to their honorary surrogate uncle.

"Long overdue indeed," he chuckled in response. "Well today ladies, in honor of your reunion, brunch is on the house. Our esteemed Executive Chef, Imani has arranged a wonderful array of delectable selections including some new items that will be featured on the exclusive menu for the upcoming First Lady's International Luncheon. So, relax and enjoy your meal as well as your time with one another. Your servers will be here momentarily."

The women were touched and genuinely appreciative. They all thanked him and raised their champagne flutes of mimosa or sparkling water to toast their brunch host, Imani.

"It is certainly my pleasure. I miss you guys so much. I mean it is not often that I am not either deep in the hustle and bustle of the kitchen or traveling. It is a treat for me to catch up in person."

"Oh, Imani we miss you too girlfriend," Denise declared. "I was so proud seeing you win that cooking show competition on TV last week...*Elite Eats.*"

"But I didn't win," replied Imani, with a look of perplexity, while almost choking on the sip of her cocktail.

"Technicality sis. Quite simply, you were robbed, "she said, countering with a matter-of-fact look accompanied by a head and eye roll before sipping her mimosa. "You shaving your head on camera like you were preparing for battle surely brought their ratings up. It went viral on the internet. And oh my goodness, the memes called Ninja Chef or Rambo Chef are hilarious, because you know when a Sista chops off her hair...it's about to be on and popping!"

"Exactly!" chimed Renee. "Besides, who wins a cooking competition, doing chicken two ways? And one of the ways was undercooked! Robbed!" Renee and Denise high-five hand slaps one another in agreement.

"He should have spent time cooking that damn chicken one way; Done!" added Octavia. They all burst into laughter. "And does anyone else hate the tag line, Chef Imani…"

"…You've been served!" they all irritably recited in unison.

"Aw. I love you all…and hell yeah, I was robbed!" The group laughed again.

"So, Tae and Nae, how is the mausoleum makeover going?" Denise joked. "I heard that there was special care given to any original carpentry removed from the Manor and taken to storage. It is really interesting that if someone ever wanted to restore the historical elements of design, they have that option. How green. People love that type of thing. Wow, you know what? I would be happy to have one of our entertainment attorneys pitch it as a reality show to the home improvement networks," joked Denise.

"Now that is not a bad idea. See Renee," replied Octavia, tossing wide eyes to Renee. "

"Girl you are so, so bad," Renee said, covering her mouth with her napkin, shaking her head, and chuckling. "But it is going better than I thought it would. I just wish…" A look of melancholy fell upon her mid-sentence.

"Oh Nae, what's wrong?" Denise reaches over and lovingly squeezes her best friend's hand.

"It's nothing. Baby hormones, I guess. I am just missing Phillip. He was supposed to be back last week and…well today, he missed our OB appointment. Tomorrow was to be our first Lamaze class," she spoke softly as her eyes began to water.

"Sweetie, foot in mouth. Had I known, I would not have joked about the house…well, I probably would have, because you know how I really feel about that place. But I love you and I would have shown some sensitivity. I really had no idea that Phillip was still in Italy. Last time we spoke, you were at the airport to pick him up. I mean, I rode with you to Logan, and you dropped me off at the outbound terminal for my business trip to LA. You said you were OK with waiting an hour for his plane to arrive from Fiumicino."

"And I was. He just never showed up. I waited for all passengers to deboard and eventually found out that he never made the flight."

"Seriously?" asked Imani

"Oh, it gets weirder," replies Octavia, who is the most up to date at the table, but equally confused."

The food arrived and it looked almost too good to eat. Each dish displayed like the cover, or full feature spread of an upscale food magazine. Renee felt that it was an opportune moment to tailor the conversation and regroup emotionally. Her friends compassionately agreed.

Both Imani and Octavia received work related calls as dessert arrived to the table. Each apologized, but had to cut the reunion short. Rainchecks and hugs were extended and accepted. Renee and Denise were able to finish the elaborate meal and finish their conversation in a way that only two who were more than best friends, more than sorority sisters, former college roommates, and secret sharing confidants could.

"Before I face cross examination, counselor, I need to give you something to hold on to for me." Renee reaches into her purse and pulls out a sealed envelope and hands it to Denise.

"What is this?" Denise asks while curiously examining the blank envelope.

"Inside of this envelope is the gender of your godchild."

"Oh, my goodness Nae. Are you asking me to be the Godmother?"

"Seriously? Like who else would it be?"

"Um?" Denise looked into the air as if she was wondering. She then laughs. "So little one, prepare to be spoiled! She said, projecting her voice towards Renee's belly. "Now, are we having a girl or boy...or should I open it?" she asked with excitement.

"Neither." Renee smirked and enjoyed toying with her bestie. She placed her hand on top of Denise's hand to stop her from opening the envelope.

"Neither? I don't understand."

"OK. OK. I will let you off the hook. I don't know the gender. I had my scheduled sonogram today and it just didn't feel right receiving the news without Phillip. I opted to have it sealed to share with him when he gets home, or perhaps one of those gender reveal parties, or at a baby shower."

"I got it, girlfriend. I'm going to put this in a safe place and will come up with a fun and creative reveal. Once Phillip comes home, we can put a plan in motion. Any idea when that will be?"

"I wish I knew."

"Renee, I do not want to sit here and dig it out of you. I need to know what is going on and I need to know right now," Denise demanded in a more serious tone than usual.

"I wish that I had answers. I really do not have an idea where Phillip is or when he is coming home. It has been a week since I last spoke with him…"

"What? A week?"

"Yes, and before you ask, no we did not have a fight. We have never been closer. In fact, he calls at least 3 times a day. He has me put the phone against my belly and he talks to our baby so that the baby can hear his voice every day, whether he is home or out of town."

"And um…there is no other woman by any chance?"

"Aw come on now Dee?"

"Well, I do have to ask. In my business, I have seen it all. But I will admit, he did win me over by being so attentive to you. So, let's try to look at this from another perspective. I know a guy who discretely handles situations for some of our firm's missing husband cases. I will give him a call.

I am going to clear my schedule for the rest of the day. We should stop by his restaurant on the way to your house. I want you to pack a bag and stay with me for a few nights until we figure this mess out. You should not be alone in that…house under construction. My godchild needs to be safe and secure."

"Dee, I can't ask you to miss work because of me. I don't know how you can handle responsibilities at your practice and the duties at the District Attorney's office. I know that you have deadlines. Hell, I have deadlines. I have so much to oversee before Phillip comes home. I will be OK."

"Renee, I want you to let me worry about work. The D.A. is always encouraging me to take some time off. I have been nonstop since joining their team after Senior's trial and conviction 2 years ago. Followed by two more high profile cases, you have just given me the push to do something different.

Calvin will be pleased mostly. And as for your deadlines Missy; I'm sure that Octavia can handle the workers and crew at your house. She is freaking Octavia Ross for God sake...and you can go over there during the day. OK? Let's just take it one day at a time. Tonight, my house. Tomorrow night, we will address it tomorrow. Agreed?"

"Agreed."

CHAPTER FOUR

There were very few things that were effective as a distraction to the worries that invaded Renee's mind lately. She continued to dive into her work remotely from home, until even she had become cognizant that she was driving both her office assistant and her personal assistant crazy. Each day that she did not hear from Phillip, her stress level raised. Although she wanted to go back to the last day that she saw him, she could not. She ventured again into the pages of the past.

Oddly enough, I still dream of cats to this very day. Most often I awake abruptly from the same recurrent dream. In my dream, a stub-tailed black cat is devouring a kitten, instead of a plump rat that is lying elegantly upon a bed of vegetables, on a fancy plate. I used to think that it was just suggestive images from the cat that I saw the night of my arrival.

I vividly recall seeing a rather large black cat that stopped in the road and stared into the headlights before disappearing into the darkness. It was something about the eyes and the stance that showed no sign of fear of the approaching vehicle casting a towering shadow over it that lingered in my thoughts. It felt as if its piercing speckled light-green eyes inventoried the interior cabin. As folklore would have it, Tom, the cat king is who I believed him to be. Never seeing him again, but his eyes I see every day in the masters of the Manor. By habit and formality, I kept my head down, but mostly because it was indeed haunting to look into the eyes of Sir Simon Mathews and even his son, Phillip.

Sir Simon Mathews, a tall, thin, pale man with a cold demeanor, has yet to speak to me directly since I arrived 2 months ago. He relies on Ethan Lee to carry out his wishes. I learned rather quickly that he was more than a chauffeur. He managed the staff and spoke on Sir Simon's behalf in both his presence and in his absence.

Young Master Phillip was not like any child I had ever known. He was more like a miniature soldier than a young boy. He had no friends, nor did he play about the house. Surprisingly, with all of the family riches, he had no toys. He only fancied a coin collection given to him by his father who was an advent collector.

Young Master Phillip was on a strict schedule, which he kept better than I did most of the time when I had first arrived. I quickly learned that this young lad frowned with distaste upon unpunctuality. It was a shared trait between him and his father who dismissed two household staff from their positions for tardiness. Being early was a practice that I never slacked on again.

CHAPTER FIVE

◆ ◆ ◆

It was a year of tragedy for the Mathews family beginning with the news that Jonathan Mathews, younger brother to Sir Simon Mathews was killed in the war, just months after their father Sir Benjamin Mathews was crippled from Polio.

Although the air of the house was somber, Madam Collins must have willed the house to run systematically that dreadful winter that she fell ill to an unknown sickness. It was evident that she was vital to the operations of the estate that she committed her woman life to service of this family. I would later find out that she was once governess to Sir Simon throughout his childhood before becoming the housekeeper of the Manor under Sir Benjamin as Master of the estate.

As I wandered the halls one evening examining the Mathews ancestry portraits, I found it rather odd that no portraits of women hung on the wall. There was a cluster of lineage oil paintings reminiscent of cemetery headstones.

I learned to move quietly on my phantom strolls to avoid discovery. It made it possible for me to quickly hide behind a column when I heard Madam Collin's bedroom door open. Surprisingly, Ethan Lee appeared. There seemed to be an air of genuine concern on his face, as I watched from the shadows, him exiting her chamber with a meal tray that looked untouched.

My heart warmed instantly even as I imagined Madam Collin's usual stoned face that was well pronounced by her pearl white hair pulled tightly back into the twisted bun slightly above the nape of her neck. Her lips were thin and barely outlined her mouth from being pressed closed. She spoke abundantly clear with her eyes, hands, and head nods of approval or disapproval. From her pristine uniform to her drawn-on eyebrows, nothing was ever out of place on her person. Even the house itself seemed to stand at attention for her daily inspection.

The only thing that was not delegated amongst capable house staff, was the care for Sir Simon's father. Although I hadn't given it much thought until that moment, Ethan must have assumed the task of caring for Sir Benjamin as well.

It was during this time that Sir Simon had retreated to his study more than usual. He began to take more frequent business trips, leaving young Phillip Mathews longing for the one human companion that he was used to, his beloved father. Phillip was not the same in his father's absence. Some days he seemed sad and withdrawn, and other days, he was angry and dark.

Phillip took pride in two things, his appearance, and his treasured coin. The coin was a 1913 Liberty Head Nickel to add to his coin collection that his father had given him. He shined that coin daily. He was never without it.

I could not understand him, but oddly, I think he did more than tolerate me. I think that he understood me better than I did him. From time to time, he handed me a variety of books from the family library to read like Hamlet and Huckleberry Finn in my spare time. It was usually one that he had just read. Sometimes I wondered who was who's companion in this equation.

Even though I did not understand this child, nor shared his enthusiasm in literature, I did understand that his father was the foundation of his entire world. Sadly, I can vividly recall the day that his world came tumbling down. It was a day that Spring was once again late.

Phillip went to his bedroom window at least twice every hour since breakfast. He sped through his lessons and returned to his post like clockwork. Eventually, I saw him fighting to contain his excitement as he peered through his bedroom window when the car pulled up in front of the Manor. He then dashed down 3 flights of stairs when he saw Ethan Lee opening the rear passenger door.

I caught up with him and stood on the landing at his side in muster with my head down looking at Phillip's face. I saw it gradually turn pale, his nares flared and the tightness in his jaw signaled that he was bearing down on his teeth. I looked up and saw Sir Simon Mathews opening the other rear car door. He extended his hand inside the doorway and out stepped a tall slender woman wearing a green wrap around coat. Her free hand was holding her matching and overly adorned doll hat in place against the fading winter winds. I could not see her full face because it was hidden behind the black net veil. But her red lipstick and auburn pin curled hair was a deep contrast against the gloomy mid-morning sky.

I covertly nudged young Phillips' shoulder to not only remind him of his manners, but to somehow absorb some of his shock and disappointment. He managed to collect himself and shook her hand when his father introduced her. I watched the three of them walk into the house and into sitting room as I stood in the foyer with the front door still open. I looked outside at Ethan Lee retrieving the rest of the luggage from the car.

I looked down at my hands. I was holding the hat of the new and official Mistress of the Manor. It was if she handed to me her crown for safe keeping without a courteous greeting. I can recall wondering if it was her or the decorative feather and florals on the hat that seemed to be most out of place?

CHAPTER SIX

Before heading to the kitchen, Denise checked in on Renee for the 3rd time since waking up. She was pleased to see that Renee was getting some sleep because she noticed that the guest bedroom light was still on in the middle of the night.

Denise was greeted by a kiss and a cup of hot coffee from her attentive husband, Calvin.

"Good morning, beautiful. How is our houseguest...or should I say guests?"

"Good morning my love. Thank you for the coffee. Mom and baby-to-be are resting. I peeked in and it looked like she must have fallen asleep reading some letters."

"Do you want a ride to the office? I will be there most of the day. I don't have any meetings at JACOM until later this afternoon."

"No babe. I am due in court mid-morning to see if I can get a continuance on a case, so I will drive. Besides, I am hoping to wrap up a few things at home before heading out."

The doorbell rang and seconds after, so did Denise's cellphone. Denise checked the caller ID on her cellphone. She blew a kiss at Calvin as he pointed to signal her that he would get the door. She took a quick sip of her coffee and headed into her study before answering the call.

"Good morning. This is Denise Rucker-Jacobs." The closing French door muffled her conversation.

Calvin could see through the tempered glass of the front door that it was a silhouette of a tall male figure on the other side. He opened the door and saw that it was David, chief investigator at the law firm.

"David, my man, come on in out of the chill. Great to see you outside of work. It's been way too long."

"Yeah buddy, they do keep me very busy. But we have to get out and catch up a bit over good whiskey, like back in the old days before you got the girl, and she made an honest man out of you." They laugh as David follows Calvin into the kitchen. "Speaking of which, is she around? I really need to speak with her."

"She's on a call right now, but she'll be right out. Just toss your coat on the back of the chair. How about a cup of coffee?"

"Sure, sounds good. Wow CJ..." David sighed and nodded his head in approval. "Married life looks good on you. You did well, friend landing brains and beauty. Come on now dude, a partner in a law firm and now Assistant District Attorney. Man, I am so glad that you decided to finally stop being a pining Clark Kent and finally showed her that you had a cape and a "big J" on your chest under that maintenance man uniform."

"Well old friend, I am a lucky man. But real talk, in hindsight, I wish that I had taken your advice sooner. But she gave me a shot despite my shenanigans. Now, when are you going to take the plunge, my guy?"

"Dude, you are looking at a blue-eyed bachelor for life... although, I thought I had met the right one a while back in Vegas at your bachelor party...oh man... a talented young lady she was. She did this thing with her..." he replied looking off into the air in a memory trance while thumb stroking his freshly shaven chin.

"Wow, would you look at the time!" Calvin said jokingly looking down at his watch to change the subject. He chugged down the last of his coffee. "You know the Vegas rule!"

"Yeah man. What happens in Vegas, stays in Vegas."

"No...Ain't no statute of limitations on stupid," he said, a decimal louder than a whisper. David gave a nod and they both smirked. "Make yourself at home. Denise should be out shortly. I gotta run, but I'll catch you later, OK?"

Before David could respond the door of the study opened and Denise came out making eye contact. She was surprised to see him this early in her home. She kissed Calvin quickly as he was hurrying off to work.

"Hey David. What brings you by this morning?"

"I wanted to catch you before you got to the office because I have some information that you asked me to look into on Phillip Mathews."

Both Denise and David abruptly turned towards the voice behind them "What about Phillip?" Renee stood in the doorway looking curious, holding her stomach. Denise moves past David towards Renee and guides her towards the bar stool at the kitchen island for her to sit.

"Good morning Nae. Come sit down. You remember David from my wedding? He works with me."

"What were you saying about Phillip?" Renee pushes Denise's helping hand away and looks into David's eyes with desperation in fear of his response. "What were you saying about my husband?" She said louder.

"I was just about to share with Denise, that I discovered that Phillip did not board the commercial flight to Italy as assumed. The flight manifest shows that a woman by the name of Sylvia St. John of Jacksonville, Florida who was on the standby list had the seat that apparently was first assigned to Phillip. She and her sister, Cheryl are both nurses who attended a medical conference here. Apparently, they had been laid over for 2 days in the airport.

I checked to see if he may have upgraded to first class since he had checked in with security. I tracked down the woman in Florida who said that two seats side by side became available 15 minutes before the gate closed. She credited her good fortune to prayer, but it left me with more questions, so I was hoping to speak to you to get information for my investigation. Was Phillip traveling alone?"

"Traveling alone? Of course, he was...I think he was. I didn't ask. I mean it was restaurant business. I don't know. Why does it matter?"

"Maybe it doesn't. I am just looking for pieces to a puzzle. It's what I do. Now on another serious note and not revealing Phillip's identity, I was talking with my buddy down at the Police Department. I am inclined to agree that due to this new information, his popularity and social standing in the community, not to mention all the publicity of his father's trial, I think that its time to file a missing persons case and get local and federal help in locating him."

Renee looked at Denise and Denise looked at Renee. They stared into each other's moist eyes and squeezed each other's hand tightly. Renee nodded to Denise. Denise walked David to the door and asked him to arrange to have his contact at the Police Department come to her home to get the process rolling.

By the end of day. Phillip Mathew's face was on both local and national news channels. Renee found it difficult to control her emotions and discovered that her emotions were in sync with the movement of their baby today. The deep breathing techniques that were to promote prenatal calmness, were not working. The only thought that she could muster was that in a matter of hours, he went from being missed to being officially missing.

CHAPTER SEVEN

Detective Marvin Twyman and his partner Detective Daniel Sneed were nicknamed BPD's Pits because with their 20 years of collective civil service and successfully closed cases, they had a reputation for not letting things go. Like prey locked in the jaws of a pit-bull, it was hard for a perpetrator to escape their clutches. They had matching artwork of growling pit-bull with handcuffs tattooed on their upper arms. The pair also raised two brother pits from the same litter that was given to them one Christmas by their wives, who coincidently are biological sisters. It is a long-standing family joke that they were the result of a double date that never ended. They were literally brothers in law. And without question, they always had each other's back.

Both Twyman and Sneed were intrigued when the missing person's case of Phillip Mathews, Jr. came across their desks, as they were the leading team in the arrest of his father, Phillip Mathews Sr.

Detective Twyman voiced to his superiors on record, that there was much more hidden in the case. He argued that if he had been given additional time, he could have uncovered it. Twyman felt that there seemed to have been such an election-season rush to get the conviction that things were left on the table. Off the record, he suspected that there were unknown powers that prevented them from uncovering the true depth of Mathews Senior's crime. He shared with his partner only that he would not be surprised if there were several well-known individuals holding shovels. Detective Sneed didn't fully rule out that assumption, but he was content with getting Senior behind bars.

As the officers of the law lay out their case, Detective Twyman is frustrated by one dead end after another. The indication caused him to be more suspicious that foul play was involved. Sneed reminded him that they were against the clock because it was only a matter of time before the Feds would snatch this high-profile case from under them.

"Okay partner let's go over the conspiracy board again. Starting with the wife, Renee Brown Mathews, still newlywed and 7 months pregnant with their first child. She is highly educated and made her name and fortune in the tech-world before marrying. The couple has a history of public legal disputes and social media break-ups and make-ups before tying the knot. Oddly, she didn't notify police of his disappearance for weeks," recites Detective Sneed.

"Don't forget to factor in that she is best friends with the A.D.A. Hell, this is the same circle that launched her career with the D.A.'s office. So, let's prepare to stomp on a pile of eggshells with that one. Now, of course you know where I'm starting. His father, Phillip Mathews, Sr. Behind bars in FMC Devens. He is sitting in that joke of a prison with a vendetta due to key witness testimony that cost him his freedom, his business holdings, and his estate where he and his wife now lives," Twyman responds, then places a red check mark beside the photograph and the name he just wrote on the dry erase board.

"Last on my list to add to the Crazy Wall is Phillip Mathews, Jr himself.

Rich guy, a former playboy, full of regrets and not ready for family responsibilities, disappears for a tropical getaway with a mistress. He probably doesn't know that he is missing and may show up in a few days with a suntan that he can't explain. I didn't see any red flags on his personal or business bank accounts. The wife said that he was traveling abroad for the restaurant. None of the staff has missed a day since his absence. The 3 Italian chefs are a little weird, arguing and singing, but the hostess, Julieta, was a looker. You never know what might be cooking there. So, I want to talk to the manager at the Wooden Spoon again to see if there are details about this so-called business trip.

I think that it would be a good idea to check out his best friend, Russell Cambridge, III. The guy inherited Phillip Senior's company...or the half of the company stolen from his father who was a business partner. I might need a scorecard to keep up with the next episode of the Rich and the Restless, but either way, he might just give us some inside information on Mathews' personal life."

"Dan let's divide and conquer, bro. How about you head over to talk to the staff and the friend? I will take the 40-mile drive to Devens. We can meet up afterwards and talk to the wife again."

"Are you sure you don't want me to go up to FMC with you?"

"No. I got this one. You are right about the time crunch. I don't mind digging up this old bone by myself. Trust me, I gnawed on it so much, I know exactly where all the nooks and crannies are."

"Then let's go dog!"

The detective duo gave each other a fist pound and let out their symbolic dog howl. The officers in the precinct looked over to observe this ritual that they all were used to seeing with these two and cheered them on as they headed to the streets.

CHAPTER EIGHT

◆ ◆ ◆

The party guests arrived in groves dressed in their finest attire. The champagne flowed and the music was festive. The Manor was alive and decorated with florals and aromas that I was not accustomed to, but I was certainly enchanted by. Boston's elite society had come to welcome the birth of Sir Simon and Mistress Mathews' son, Elliot.

I had assumed my new role in apprenticeship housekeeping under the tutelage of Madam Collins. She was physically only a fraction of her prior self before the illness. She tired easily, but her mind was still intact. The position called for discretion to be of duty as much as it was organizing chores. Madam Collins said that one must be the guardian of the generation of secrets at all costs.

I have accepted that one day I would inherit the full responsibility just as Madam did for Sir Benjamin Mathews, his late wife Catherine, and 2 sons, Simon and Jonathan, then to Simon, his late wife, Amanda, and son, Phillip. Now with a second wife, Dorothy, Sir Simon Mathews and their newborn son, Elliot. With the early death of the women of the house before their children reached adolescent age, Madam Collins has been the only constant female but certainly not a maternal figure in the Manor. That appeared to me to be an obsolete and unwelcomed role.

I still served as Au Pair to Young Master Phillip who desired and required less of my time for supervision and companionship. He was withdrawn and distant most days. He had not eaten a meal with his father in months, nor did Sir Simon call for him to join in attendance to dine with him and his stepmother.

Young Phillip had begun sleepwalking more once his father remarried. It was so frequent that Sir Simon ordered that his son's bedroom door be locked after he had been put to bed. This stemmed from an incident occurring the first week as newlyweds in the Manor when the couple awakened to Phillip standing at the foot of their bed.

I occasionally spotted him in the hallways on my secret night strolls. I would watch from the shadows as he would enter random rooms and just stand there then return to his room. I thought not much of it, but I would follow him to make sure that he did not fall to harm and would tuck him back in.

Although I laid out his tuxedo for the party, I highly doubted that he would make an appearance. Phillip no longer sought his father's approval as he once did before he remarried. I felt that his jealousy and disappointment would deter his presence and support of his newborn brother and stepmother. I had no words that would influence him at this point other than it would make Sir Simon proud to have his older son present and by his side as a united family before the important people of this town.

I did not judge anyone. I had my own series of secrets. Ethan Lee and I had begun spending time together. We took walks and talked for endless amounts of time about books and nature, stars, politics, and religion. I grew fond of him. He was such an intelligent man. He was well spoken for a man who rarely spoke. We both were fully aware that Sir Simon would not take kindly to our budding relationship, so we were invisible to one another during the day, but met like 2 thieves in the night to steal cherished moments.

The party was in full swing. At first glance, there were no smiles that seemed out of place, until surprisingly my eyes fell upon Young Master Phillip. He was present and appeared to be happy. I had never seen him in this manner. It was almost eerie.

I was replenishing refreshments when I noticed the baby nurse standing at the top of the stairs with Ethan Lee. She seemed shaken with her hands over her mouth. She was in tears. She appeared to have been directed back to the nursery.

I traced Ethan Lee's movements with my eyes as he met Madam Collins midway on the stairs. They exchanged words briefly. I observed next, Ethan Lee whispering something to Sir Simon that made him instantly turn pale. The two men hurried to the staircase.

Madam Collins was seen walking up the stairs with Dr.

Arnold, the family physician who was a party guest. He had his black medical bag in his hand. With no one else noticing anything outside of the music, dancing, and champagne, I was compelled to slip away from the distraction to follow and listen at the door of the nursery. I could not hear them clearly over the cries from the nurse.

I could not actually recall physically walking into the room, but I realized that I was in the middle of the nursery staring at the doctor holding a limp blue infant in the palm of his hand. I was frozen and invisible. I began to see that things were happening around me slower than in real time and in silence. Sir Simon had his head buried in his hands. Madam Collins was escorting the nurse out of the room, and I suspected out of the house because she put her coat over her shoulders.

I think that I took in one more deep breath which seemed like it would be my final breath, when the doctor opened the mouth of the infant and pulled out a shiny object. It sparkled when the light of the room hit it. Doctor Arnold handed the object to Ethan Lee who looked at it for a split second and placed it in his trouser pocket. He looked directly into my eyes, and I somehow knew.

I walked down the stairs, and my eye caught glimpse that Phillip was still being the pleasant little boy among the guests in celebration. I did not recognize this happy boy.

Although the guests were told that Sir Simon Mathews

was not feeling well and would retire for the evening, it was insisted that they continue to enjoy food and drinks; however, social etiquette demanded guests politely disperse, calling the festive evening to an end.

There was never discussion between Madam Collins, Ethan Lee, or myself regarding the events in the nursery the night of the party. Phillip was sent to boarding school days later. Mistress Mathews would have two still born births over the next three years and eventually went mad and stopped eating until she died of a broken heart. The Manor would never be as alive as it was the night of baby Elliot's death.

CHAPTER NINE

Russell had just left his fifth unanswered voice message in the past 3 weeks for Phillip when his secretary knocked on his office door. She stuck her head in to see if he was available. He waved her in and disconnected his call. She handed him a business card belonging to a Detective Daniel Sneed of the Boston Police Department. She had already escorted him to the conference room away from the reception area or within ear distances of the executive offices as their company practice would have her do with all guests who did not have an appointment. As he stood to exit his office, Russell requested that all calls be held for 20 minutes, then to interrupt and pull him away for an important meeting.

"Detective Sneed. Hi I'm Russ Cambridge. I hope you weren't waiting too long."

"Not at all. I was just enjoying the impressive view of the city from 42 floors up. It looks like you can tell when the Turnpike is backed up before heading home."

"Yes. there is certainly a level of traffic advantage from that window. But how can I help you, Detective?"

"I'm sorry, I know you're a busy man, so I'll be brief. I am investigating the whereabouts of Mr. Phillip Mathews, Jr. I understand that you two are friends?"

"Yes Detective, we are good friends. Since childhood."

"Can you tell me the last time you spoke to him?"

"It's been a few weeks. We went out for drinks. I think it was a day or two before his Italy trip."

"Hmm drinks. Did he seem to be in an unusual headspace?"

"Unusual? I don't understand the question."

"Let me rephrase that. Did Mathews mention over drinks with you if there was specifically anything bothering him, like business? His home life? His wife?"

"No, he didn't. And from where I stand, his life looks pretty freaking good. Besides, I am his friend and not his therapist."

"That's interesting. So, was he seeing a therapist?"

"Not that anything is wrong with it, but I think so. If you had a father like Senior, you would need to talk to someone too. The creep did a number on him and a whole lot of other people in this town."

Russell's secretary entered the conference room on cue and alerted her employer that he was needed for an important meeting in the conference room next door. She mentioned with emphasis that the client and other team members were seated and waiting. Both Russell and the detective could see through the wall of the glass enclosed room that they were in, that another glass enclosed conference room across the hall was occupied with people sitting around a table. Russell excused himself and extended his hand for a handshake.

"Thank you for your time, Mr. Cambridge, but one more question before you run off. Would you happen to know who Phillip is seeing...ah, do you know who his therapist is?"

"I'm sorry, but you may want to check with his wife, Detective Sneed. Have a good rest of your day."

CHAPTER TEN

Renee opened her eyes to the blurry view of Phillip's dreamy blue eyes and perfect smile. As her vision became more in focus, she realized that it was just the framed photograph that sat on her bedside table. It was her favorite wedding photo. She panned out to see herself in the picture. She smiled briefly, then turned over to see his empty side of the bed, where his pillow was fluffed and undisturbed. Before the tears could fully develop, she felt the pressure on her bladder prompting her to get up and race to the bathroom.

She could hear her cell phone ringing from a distance as she washed her face in front of the bathroom mirror. She decided to let it go to voicemail while she finished her morning hygiene, followed by the second trip to the water closet to empty her bladder. It suddenly dawned on her after hearing the back-to-back calls, that someone wanted to urgently reach her. She thought for a split second that it may even be Phillip and ran to the bed to grab her phone regretting that she made herself unavailable, even if it was just for a few minutes.

"Hello! Hello!" she yelled into the phone, then paused before experiencing a sense of disappointment. "No Russell. It's not a bother," she said and paused to listen. "I appreciate you calling to check on me and don't think I don't realize that you have been added to the mommy-babysitting duty rotation. I love you for it and will see you later."

Renee hit the cancel button to disconnect the call, then took a long look around her bedroom. She pondered on how she once thought that she would never fully embrace living in Mathews Manor, yet alone calling it her home. But as the final touches are underway, combined with all the work that Octavia and her team have incorporated were more than adequate. The house design read spectacular and magical. Even Denise had admitted that the changes were nothing short of what she termed, a designer's exorcism. She comfortably spent the last few nights at the Manor to give Renee the opportunity to be in a place where she felt closer to Phillip.

Renee placed the tin box of journaling letters in her dresser drawer. The loose page diaries confirmed that Mathews Manor is a dwelling that had just received a facelift, but undoubtably, the skeletal bones were still very much there.

Renee opted to use the newly installed elevator for the first time. She felt comfortable using it since she was not home alone. Entering the kitchen, Renee gasped at the sight of the individual with broad shoulders seated at the kitchen table, wearing a Red Sox baseball cap turned backwards, reading cell phone messages.

"Oh my God! Where the hell have you been?" She shouted walking closer to the table. She stopped 2 feet short of reaching him with her hand extended to grab him, when he turned around to face her. It was not Phillip as she instinctively thought. She did not know who this man was. She looked perplexed as she tried to catch her breath. Octavia walked into the kitchen and handed the gentleman an envelope.

"Thanks again Jason. I will let you see yourself out. We can finalize the rest of the plans on Thursday," Octavia said hastily before turning to Renee and grabbing her shoulders. "Renee... you alright? You don't look well...hmm, come sit down. I hope that we didn't disturb you. I specifically instructed my team to not start anything loud until Noon." Octavia guided Renee to the chair that her new project manager, Jason was just sitting in.

"Oh no. I'm OK. I just...um, I just could use some tea," she chuckled and recovered to mask the awkward moment.

"Sure thing. I already have a kettle on. I still love that even with all these space-age type of kitchen gadgets in here, there is an old-fashioned kettle and porcelain tea set. It reminds me so much of our tea dates back in the day and our girl trip to England…yes, the Brit Studs are my cup of tea. Oh, oh I brought over this gift basket of the tea and treats assortment Imani had delivered to you this morning. She said it was full of your favorites." Octavia picked up the beautifully wrapped basket and handed it to Renee. Her eyes brightened, followed by a genuine smile at the gourmet delectables presented to her.

Denise walked into the kitchen wearing black plush slippers and a matching plush bathrobe over her satin pajamas. Her head was wrapped in a tan terry cloth turban protecting her hair line from the avocado-colored paste on her face. Renee and Octavia both look at her, then look at each other and burst out laughing. Denise amusingly held in her laughter and ignored them and headed over to the cabinet and retrieved a coffee cup before heading to the coffee maker.

"Renee, check your gift basket to see if Imani threw in some tortilla chips. Denise may need something to go with the guacamole she's wearing," joked Octavia. The three of them laugh. Denise sips her cup then pretends to try to kiss Octavia with her masked face that sends her running to the opposite side of the kitchen to avoid getting her blush button down cashmere sweater soiled.

"I wish that I could hang out with you natural beauties today, but I am going to head to the office for a few meetings and have lunch with my handsome husband, if I am lucky," Denise announced.

"Dee, why don't you go home and spend time with Calvin

tonight. I am sure he misses you. I'll be fine."

"You can't get rid of me, roomie. Calvin is more than on board, so it's my place or yours until Phillip gets back. Besides, I take my Godmother duties seriously and I plan to stick close to this little one until he or she makes their grand entrance," Denise said matter-of-factly as she grinned and patted Renee's rounded belly.

"Godmother? Alright now, did I miss the memo or meeting? And yes, I know that I don't do ki..ki..kids, but I have you both know that I was once a child and I will make an exception for this love bundle." Denise and Renee laughed.

"Tae, you know it takes a village and you are an Auntie...No, you are the Auntie of aunties," Renee confirmed.

"Queen of the Aunties!" Denise expounded,

"Now, I like the sound of that!" The three laughed. Denise blew them a kiss and leaves to get dressed.

"Now that I have you alone sis..." Octavia spoke slowly and cautiously. "I want to talk to you about completing the nursery." Octavia placed a piping hot cup of tea in front of Renee.

"No Tae! I told you! I am going to wait until Phillip comes home so that he can be a part of it."

"Please don't get upset with me. I am only trying to help. I just thought that with most of the work nearing completion, the nursery can be a distraction."

"A distraction from what?"

"You know...Phillip...I mean the tabloids and..."

"I don't need a distraction from my husband, Octavia! And if I lived my life based on the tabloids, I would have lost my mind a long time ago. What I need is…What I need is for him to come home to us," she wept and started a full-fledged cry.

Octavia wrapped her arms around Renee to comfort her sobbing friend. She apologized with sincerity and realized that Renee's tears were from a much deeper place than a response to her suggestion. They sat for 15 minutes holding each other's hand in silence, except the intermittent sniffles that eventually became sporadically infrequent.

The doorbell rang twice. Octavia suggested that Renee drink her tea while she went to see who was at the front door.

Thinking that it may be a delivery of some sort, Octavia was surprised and devilishly amused by the attractive visitor standing in the doorway.

"Well, well, well. Mr. Russell Cambridge the third," she said in a sultry seductive voice.

"Ms. Octavia Love-em and Leave-em Ross. You are even more gorgeous than the last time I saw you. My heart breaks again just looking at you."

"Oh, you lie like a Persian rug. But come on in anyway. I like the way you lie."

"If that was in fact true, then you would have called me back or even an anniversary text or email."

"Look Loverboy, the champagne at Renee and Phillip's wedding reception was playing matchmaker and we both got caught up in curiosity and the heat of the moment or…moments if I recall correctly."

"So, at least I see that neither of us have forgotten. I guess I just have to settle for that. Right?"

"Maybe a discussion for another time, Russell Cambridge the third. I am certain that you didn't come here to see me, so let me take you into the kitchen."

"Please do. Please do."

Renee rose from the table and went over to hug Russell. Their arms held tight as their hearts pressed together to exchange unspoken concern. Russell cleared his throat to gather his composure.

"Renee...the place looks fantastic. I mean, I grew up coming over here and it was always like something locked in the past...but not in a bad way. This is some next level something else. Who has a full on Tuscan Chef's kitchen and an everyday sleek kitchen connected by a butler's pantry. Yeah, now who does that?"

"Well, my designer knows her stuff," she grinned, then looked over at Octavia.

"I'm sure she does...I mean, I can see that she is extremely talented," he says, staring at Octavia. Look um...can we talk for a minute. I had a visit from a Detective Dan Sneed with questions about Phillip. Mainly about you and Phil..."

"Oh, that is my cue. I think I hear my crew arriving. I will leave you two to talk privately. Nice seeing you again Mr. Cambridge." Octavia adjusted her clothing and wiggled towards him to pass him as she exited the kitchen.

"The pleasure is all mine. Please call me...Russell," he said and winked.

CHAPTER ELEVEN

Undeniably, patience was not his strong suit. 90-minutes of pacing outside of the warden's office while being stared at by a correctional officer and two inmates who kept moping the same area of the floor started to irritate him.

Detective Twyman could not shake his feelings that many unanswered questions and cold cases around Boston always led to the backyard or in the vicinity of Phillip Mathews, Sr. He also thought it no coincidence that life in a minimum-security prison was quickly supported by questionable judiciary officials. He stood by his suspicions that there was a brotherhood in play that supported a ring of fire around a band of thieves. But he knew that saying it to the wrong person at the wrong time would jeopardize his advantage of investigating under a facade. He believed that the more comfortable a crook gets, the more careless they operated. Twyman did not care that he did not have an appointment prior to coming to the prison and he was prepared to sit on the uncomfortable floor mounted 5-beam seating for another 90-minutes if needed.

When a dark silhouette filled the frosted opaque window panel of the door behind the black lettering, Warden John Floyd, Detective Twyman stood up and watched the door slowly open inward and a short stout balding man with a red beard resting on his chest steps out. He had his face buried in a ledger. He removed his glasses and looked up at the C.O. and nodded some signal known only between them before even acknowledging the law enforcement officer in his waiting area. After the inmates and correctional officer made their way further down the corridor, the Warden looked at Twyman, then invited him into his office.

Marvin noticed the oversized desk in front of the window with a panoramic view of the camp and adjacent medical facility. He was surprised to see that only a computer monitor, a land line telephone and the ledger that he was just holding were the only items on the desk. The shine on the immaculate wood surface had a reflection of the treetops and lamps from light posts around the compound.

As the warden took his position behind his desk and sat in his brown high-back leather swivel chair, the detective assessed the numerous framed photographs on the wall. There was the warden with two consecutive Mayors of both Devens and Boston, the warden side by side with the current State Governor, and the warden shaking hands with the Vice-President of the United States of America. It resembled either a cheap diner's wall of fame or an attempt at picture name dropping. Regardless of which, Detective Twyman was unimpressed.

"Quite the impressive photo collection you have here, Warden."

"Thank you...detective?"

"Detective Marvin Twyman, Sir. BPD."

"You are a long way out of your jurisdiction Detective Mark Twyman of BPD; and without an appointment. How can I be of assistance to you?"

"Yes Warden, I apologize for the inconvenience. I'm working on a case and wanted to speak to one of your inmates, specifically Phillip Mathews, Sr., but I couldn't get clearance at the visitation desk. I was told that perhaps you could help me bypass some red tape."

"Red tape?"

"Yeah, you know the red tape of getting a court order to be

released into my custody and be transported to the precinct for questioning. Are you aware that his son is missing?"

"So, is this an official notification or an investigation?"

"Now that depends. I will know which one when I speak with him."

"Well detective, if you are not on the approved visitor's list and the inmate's attorney isn't present, then you may just have to explore your red tape options." The warden stood up and walked to the door in a dismissive fashion. When he opened the door, there stood a tall dark skinned African American correctional officer with both hands behind his back. He was tight lipped and had a serious blank stare. He was so muscular that his physique was intimidating. "It would appear that our business here is done, Detective. Sergeant Washington will show you out. In the meantime, I will utilize my reliable connections to make sure that Inmate Mathews is constantly updated with any information regarding his son."

Detective Twyman took another quick look around the room inhaling and taking every detail in, then he did a series of nods with a bluff of a smirk on his face. He stood in the doorway nose to nose with the correctional officer as the warden looked on.

"Nice biceps Washington. You may want to go up in size on that government issued uniform unless it's just a dress-to-impress an inmate thing?" I look forward to seeing you when I come back." He winked at the warden and adjusted his necktie and the outward facing leather wallet displaying his gold detective shield clipped to the belt around his waist.

After watching the Detective exit the prison from the live camera feed on his desktop monitor. The warden picked up his cellphone and hit a programmed number.

"I can't buy any more time. You have 72 hours to get back and clean up all loose ends leading back to me or the organization or you can add yourself to the body count."

CHAPTER TWELVE

As intended, the unpaved road was not at all inviting. It was rocky and uncomfortable to say the least, but it was a shortcut that saved thirty minutes off his commute to his hidden gem, a cozy cabin getaway.

Kenny was skillful at maneuvering his 4-wheeldrive with all-terrain tires right up to the property entrance which was covered with overgrown brush that blocked access to the path. It did not however obscure the keep out and no trespassing on private property signs affixed to the chained wooden gate.

Exiting the vehicle, Kenny put on a pair of mirrored lens sunglasses then looked up and gave a quick glance at the camera anchored to the pole 12 feet above ground level. The motion sensor camera was activated by his movement. The lens followed him over to the gate where he unlocked the heavy-duty, stainless-steel chain that was weaved through the gate. He then walked over to the wood post where there was a camouflaged door panel embedded in the pole. He depressed the door , revealing a keypad. Kenny entered 4 numbers and pressed the pound button, which activated the electronic cantilever gate to open. He hurriedly re-entered his black range rover that disappeared into the wooded background as the remaining foliage of the season covered the gate that closed behind him. The camera shifted again, capturing him moments later locking the chain and returning into the brush.

After a mile drive, the cabin came into full view. Kenny inhaled deeply to slow his heart rate. He almost allowed his mind to slip back to a moment in time when this was his haven of refuge, relaxation, and peace of mind to escape the complexities of a long Operating Room shift rotation. But in the last year and a half, any nostalgic memories attached to this dwelling were unfortunately replaced with pre-calculated strategic protective measures.

Three barking rottweilers appeared suddenly running from the side of the house into the garage surrounding the vehicle as the engine stopped. Kenny sat still for a moment after catching his reflection in the rear-view mirror. He stared into his own eyes as if he was in search of a glimpse of his soul which he thought would more than likely be attached to a sold merchandise tag.

The exterior sounds were muffled. Although he was fully aware of the canine serenade, it was the thump on the window from heavy paws that released him from a semi-trance state. Kenny exited the rover noticing the wagging tails of his boys, a trio of rotties. After giving a command of greeting formation, he gave each a petting hug, a paw high five, and a treat that he pulled from his jacket pocket. He looked away from the dogs and watched the garage door close fully before heading inside.

Kenny removed his baseball cap and shades and placed them on the kitchen counter along with his keys. He peered into the living room and noticed Tonya's curly chestnut brown hair hanging over the back of the rocking chair that suggests that it was still damp from a shower. This is what her hair looked like when she had not dry-blown it out yet. He could see her slippers near the bottom of the chair, but not her feet. She was curled up in front of the large picture window with her knees nestled against her chest. He started towards her but stopped. He thought it best not to start the evening in disguise.

As the shower ran and slowly began to form steam in the bathroom, he stood naked at the sink and looked into the mirror. He reached across his face and pinched up the corner of his beard right below his jaw line and pulled softly until he felt a release.

He continued to pull until the fake beard fully detached from his skin, leaving a residue of glue behind. He repeated the steps until the fake mustache was removed. The steam that filled the room covered the mirror, but he did not wipe. He continued the task at hand then stepped into the hot shower awaiting him.

Resting his palms against the wet tiled shower wall, Kenny closed his eyes as the stress of the day...the stress of the week began to swell up inside of him like lava inside of a volcano looking for an escape exit. He squeezed his eyes tighter to rustle up enough strength to push it all back down to the depth of his core into a place of forgetfulness. It wasn't until he felt the contour of soft curves pressing into his back and the tight embrace that clutched his torso ever so tightly that he would yield to his burdening emotions. He was locked into a continuous squeeze until his body began to quake. The rumble of shivers found an opening in the glands of his tear ducts inevitably forcing the pressure to part his pressed lips. Tonya comforted his sadness until all his manly cries washed down the drain.

CHAPTER THIRTEEN

Denise checked in on Renee and was relieved that her friend had finally fallen asleep after the ordeal of the evening. When she went to adjust the throw blanket over her for comfort, she noticed a pile of letters in a tin box and several loose pages on the bed. Denise saw that they looked old and that intrigued her. As she began to read them, she grew even more interested. She paused to collect them from around Renee's sleeping body.

Moving over to the chaise lounge chair situated in the corner of Renee's bedroom, Denise organized them and began to read as many as she could in chronological order up to the page retrieved from Renee's hand that she must have been reading when she dozed off.

Sir Simon grew as bitter as the day was long. He began to drink heavily. He did not allow Phillip to come home for holiday for his first 3 years at Milton.

I suspect that is one of the reasons for his behavior problems. Fortunate for Phillip, the Mathews' name carries enough prestige for the school to be more tolerant; however, it was feared that he would bring a level of embarrassment to the family that would taint their aristocratic popularity more so than when he remarried six months after burying his second wife.

But as the thief in the night that she was, it would appear that her sins had caught up with her on a dark road with her lover and legal husband behind the wheel of her automobile crashed into a tree. He still sits in jail to this day claiming that he swerved the car to avoid a very large black cat with glowing eyes that appeared out of nowhere.

Cash, jewels, and family heirlooms recovered from the trunk of the vehicle were returned to Sir Simon's attorney. I am sure that she, who shall remain nameless, was buried in an unmarked grave at Widow's Cape on the Hill, since it was easier to bury the truth, than make a public spectacle of this matrimonial farce.

To leave sleeping dogs and napping bears alone, was the lesson that I soon learned in a very harsh manner. My role was to keep the secrets of the Mansion and not become a part of them regardless of good intentions.

I will never forget the fury in the eyes of Sir Simon Mathews before I nearly lost consciousness. Ethan Lee managed to wrestle him off of me, releasing his grip from around my neck that nearly snapped my windpipe in two. It was the middle of the night when I had been discovered in Sir Simon's private study using his typewriter.

I could not readily find any words that could logically explain why I was there in his study, yet alone what it was that I was doing. I moved slowly away from his desk as he approached me. I held my breath and watched him walk over to the desk. He turned the cylinder knob releasing the sheet of paper from the carriage and stood there reading the words that I had orchestrated. I could literally see the rage build within him right before he reached for me with one hand, like a cobra strike. I had not fully thought out how this ruse would end, because I was in too deep.

All I knew was that no matter what the cost, I could never close off my heart to Phillip. I was hired to be his companion and for years, he was in fact mine. My decision to impersonate his father in correspondence was to give Phillip what he needed while separated from who he cherished most and what I thought someday would be what his father needed as well. It also gave me an opportunity to covertly stay informed on his wellbeing while he was away in boarding school.

Surprisingly, my employment was not terminated immediately; however, the punishment accepted was harsh and cruel as I was forced to openly reveal my deception to Phillip during his first visit back to the Manor, at the gravesite of his grandfather's funeral. His father, my benefactor, walked off leaving me standing in confession with Phillip in the rain.

My tears fell onto the earth. They dissipated into the foreign land that was now my home. The soil that covered the family patriarch of 3-generations was hydrated and nourished with my sorrow. Little did I know then that they would share a common focus of hate and that the wrath of both father and son would fall upon me for years to come.

CHAPTER FOURTEEN

Dr. Kenneth Bailey laid in bed staring at the ceiling while next to the warm naked body of the woman he loved. Although the hypnotic aroma of their shared passion remained in the air, he could not stop thinking desperately of how to get them both out of this situation. He had tried to no avail on several occasions to escape the clutches of his tormentor, but his window of opportunity and options always disappeared along with his confidence. At this moment he feared most that he was running out of time. He thought if there was in fact a chance to put an end to his nightmare, he needed to find an answer quickly. He believed that the answer lay in the room next door.

He mentally revisited his activities to secure covering his tracks besides securing his cabin hideaway titled to the name of one of his terminal patients. He always parked in the hospital parking garage in one car, then he would put on his disguise, then take the shuttle bus to the hospital visitor's parking garage to the AWD that was cash purchased and registered to another patient who was incapacitated. Kenny had engaged in several behavior patterns over 2 years as not to arouse suspicion that he was hiding money. He made routine cash withdrawals from his bank account and in the event, he was being followed. Kenny wanted to be seen frequenting the dog track, gentleman's club, or any place that would give the impression that he was splurging away the cash, rather than pocketing the money to support life on the run. He often pretended to be drunk whenever he left the bars and strip clubs even though he spent hours drinking club soda. He wished that he could sleep comfortably anywhere outside of the surgeon's sleeping lounge, but watching Tonya sleep gave him some comfort. Slipping from under her arm that rested across his chest without disturbing her was another task that he achieved for the day.

Kenny checked the security monitors and reviewed the feed of the past 8 hours in fast forward mode after feeding the dogs and refreshing their water bowls. He went into the spare bedroom to check on his patient and was pleased to see that the surgical incision looked well underneath the freshly applied bandage. The telemetry monitor showed that all vital signs were stable and that there were no signs of infection. Tonya entered the dimly lit bedroom as Kenneth was checking his patient's pupil reactions with a pen light. She walked over to the bedside to be supportive or to assist in any way required.

"How is he?"

"His recovery is going well. You've done a great job taking care of him."

"Thanks. Sylvia and Cheryl taught me well. They are so fond of you, Kenny and would do anything to help you."

"The feeling is certainly mutual. I will miss them but knowing that they will soon learn that they have been set up for their dream retirement life in the Keys for their risks and dedication gives me some comfort. I will just be glad when this nightmare is finally over."

"Will it ever be over?"

"I am hoping that this part of it will be. But it all depends on him. He is the missing key to our plans. I know that I put our plans at risk, but I just couldn't let him die at the hands of those butchers."

"You saved my life Kenny...and you saved his."

"What about those who I couldn't save, like your brother? Like my brother?"

"Don't do this, baby. It was my fault what happened to Bryant, not yours. He was looking for me. He wanted to save me. That is what he had been doing for most of my life. I sometimes feel like I don't deserve happiness; like I don't deserve you. You saved my life even after your brother and I pulled you in this situation. You don't deserve a life on the run and always looking over your shoulder.

"Let's go into the living room, Tonya." Kenny lovingly grabbed a hold of her hands and led her into the living room and onto the sofa. He kissed the back of her head and nestled her oversized-shirt covered body against his bare chest and cuddled her with his muscular arms.

"If things work out the way I've planned it, with some adjustments, of course, we won't have to look over our shoulders much longer," he says as he runs his fingers through her long loose curls.

"Kenny, it seems like every time we get close to escaping this nightmare, we end up still running further away. I don't think that I know how to dream anymore," Tonya said hopelessly with a tear trail."

"Close your eyes and imagine a villa surrounded by lush green foliage with your own art studio filled with one masterpiece after another. Invision us taking morning walks on a pure white sandy beach and spending endless hours in secluded waterfalls. Imagine being the wife of a village physician adored and protected by the local children and their families. Image you and I and our boys sailing away to our freedom. You can see it babe, right? Babe?

Kenny looked down and moved Tonya's hair from her face and noticed that she had fallen into a peaceful sleep. He looked over at the boys sprawled across the rug in front of the fireplace. They too were napping with their paws touching each other. Kenny allowed the cushions to continue to cradle them as he reached behind him and grabbed the plaid throw blanket beside him and tossed it across the two of them. "Go ahead and dream my love because doing the right thing for the right people is our ticket to escape the wrong done for the wrong people," he said before closing his eyes.

CHAPTER FIFTEEN

From the back seat of the executive luxury car, Renee laid her head back against the headrest and admired the city lights. She had just satisfied her craving for sushi, during an elegant dinner and an entertaining evening with Octavia. The two cordially made an appearance at an art gallery downtown to support Sasha's new beau who was the featured artist. They both thought him to be extremely talented, and that his work would show well in both modern and eclectic environments. Octavia gave him her business card and they spoke of the possibility of commissioning a piece for one of her NYC clients.

Although Renee began to feel somewhat tired, it was Denise's call asking them to meet her at the Manor for their last slumber party before Octavia's flight out that would bring the night on the town to an end.

The ladies kicked off their shoes and granted their toes freedom. Octavia coaxed Renee to position herself on the seat and place her swollen feet on her lap. She complied and sighed with welcomed relief that she did not know she needed.

"Tonight was so much fun. I can't remember the last time I was out at night. The nights that Phillip didn't work late at the restaurant, he preferred to relax and chill as much as possible underneath the rubble and havoc of reno-ville. So, thank you for this. I am sure going to miss you being here Tae," she said with sincerity as she reached to grab Octavia's hand and clench their fingers together in their sisterly bonding grasp.

"No thank you for making me your plus one for the art show. I made a few connections that I am looking forward to exploring once I get back from Paris."

"Off to another adventure you go," Renee sighed. "I miss traveling too...Holland in the springtime is probably my favorite place and time. So, Tae...tell me, do you ever dream of what it might be like to find your special person? You know the one who will make you throw caution to the wind and take a chance at the altar?"

"Never and no. Girl, I am a romance addict! Romantics like me are meant to be loved, adored, and sought after. Romance is the events that occur before marriage and after divorce, that is if you are lucky not to have been stripped bone dry of passion. Romance ends somewhere between the honeymoon and the final payment to the creditors for the fairytale wedding. I just choose to live a romantic lifestyle. I have seen far more than my share of couples spending half of their marriage trying to rekindle the fire with a pack of wet matches, like date night and role playing," she says with a yawning gesture. "And honey, nothing amuses me more than people who drag an unwilling partner to counseling sessions as a last ditch effort to prolong the inevitable. Nope girl...I'm good."

"Alrighty then. I think I get your drift...again. And I know you joke a lot about not wanting children, but have you ever thought what it would be like to have a family of your own someday?"

"Nope. I am so satisfied with being crowned the best Auntie and Co-Vice-Godmother ever, thank you. But on a serious note, I need you to know that you all are my family. The family that I have created. And it gets bigger each time one of you marries or multiplies," she laughs. "Besides, parenting requires selfless sacrifice. We both know that isn't me. I look at it as if I am sparing the world of contaminated genes just in case darkness skips a generation."

"Stop it Tae you are selfless and so giving! I have always been able to see past the fashion designed and hard exterior persona well into your squishy soft insides," she chuckled, then paused more seriously. "Do you really think that darkness is hereditary?" she asks in a tone of concern while rubbing her round belly. Octavia noticed and quickly tried to pivot and recant her last statement.

"Oh no Renee. You know that I am no expert on genealogy, and I really don't mean to project my dysfunctional childhood on you. I have rebranded myself into this specimen of fabulousness. It is my own fear of not getting motherhood right that I can't entertain the thought," she paused to gather herself from a moment of transparency. "Look, you have so much good in you darling that it would cancel out any negative spirit that comes within 6 feet of you."

"So, do you think your views on marriage are out of fear too?"

"Aw hell no. That is a real-real thang girlfriend! Tried and true." Both Renee and Octavia broke out in laughter.

"Tae you are a mess, a lovely mess. I know that I keep saying this, but I am going to miss you so much. I can't believe it will all be wrapped up in a few days and then you will be off to your next adventure."

"I will be back in Manhattan in 2 weeks. New York is not that far, and I can certainly come back here to Boston as soon as you and Phillip are ready to finalize the nursery plans. We can also video chat before the baby shower or gender reveal party. The nursery can be completed in a weekend since all the prep work was done."

"About that," chimed Renee. "I know that I sort of freaked out before when you brought up the topic of the nursery, but I was wondering if there was a chance that we could change one of the other guestrooms into a nursery instead and perhaps turn the old nursery into a storage room, powder room or upper-level laundry room."

"Well, there is no plumbing in the nursery and the baby will be here long before the permits and inspections would be done. But you can never have too much storage. It can be seasonal clothes closet for winter wear. It wouldn't take much time to turn one of the fabulous, designed rooms into a nursery. I can get the designs done by tomorrow and keep it baby neutral to give you and Phillip a blank slate to decorate."

"Thanks Tae, you don't know how relieved I am about that." she sighed. Octavia looked puzzled.

"I don't want to pry, but is there a reason for the change of heart?"

"Well, there is something about it being a nursery since the house was built and I want to make it my own here. I want our child to begin life free of any stigmas attached to the history of this house," Renee concluded, convincing her friend that there was nothing more to the motives of her decision. Convincing herself that the diary pages of Elizabeth Betterton played no role in her decision, would be much more challenging.

The day before Madam Collins passed away, she gave me a beautiful tin box that contained a locket and a bundle of her memoirs as caregiver to the Mathews family.

My role of secret keeper lends me to leave her story as hers to tell. I will leave the pages buried beneath my own, revealing only the portions that pertain to me.

In her words, history would have it that Madam Freda Collins' blind loyalty to this family was rooted in love, love for Benjamin Mathews. I question if those feelings were reciprocated, since he repeatedly married and had affairs with other women.

Even with all of that, she proved that she would still do anything for him, even if it was of a despicable nature. He and only what mattered to him did she take care of. That would include giving away a child she bore for him. A daughter that she laid no eyes on for over 18 years of her life. A daughter that with her last breath, she did not even acknowledge as the bastard Mathews child, discarded to a British orphanage. May the Lord have mercy on the madness of souls, for on this day, On Half-Quarter Hill, lies the bones of the Winter Equinox Queen, mother to the lost Spring Solstice Princess.

CHAPTER SIXTEEN

The smell of fried potatoes and onions stimulated Kenny's olfactory, awakening him from a deep sleep on the sofa. Potato hash was certainly his favorite guilty pleasure comfort meal. He opened his eyes and laid there for a moment watching Tonya move about the kitchen and imagined a few ways to burn off the calories he would soon consume. The aroma of freshly brewed coffee made him toss off the blanket and announce to his woman and to the world that he was rested and rejuvenated.

After pouring himself a half a cup of hot coffee, he sipped it to wash away the breath of the night from his jaws and tongue before greeting Tonya with a kiss to the nape of her neck. He quickly reviewed the security monitors and walked onto the porch to take in the crisp New England air and watched the boys roam around the grass to relieve themselves before he headed in to do the same.

Kenny showered, then devoured breakfast and Tonya before showering again. As he pulled his Patriot's NFL sweatshirt down over his head, Tonya, with a look of urgency, hurriedly entered their bedroom, requesting that he come to the guest bedroom to assess his patient; to which he complied with haste.

"He is moaning as if he was trying to talk."

"Thank you. I got it from here."

Tonya looked on as Kenny adjusted the I.V. fluid volume and dabbed a moist towel to the patient's lips, before manually opening his eye lids and shining the pen light into his eyes again. The patient became more responsive with increased head movement.

"It looks like someone is coming around. Hey buddy. Can you hear me?"

The patient's eyes flutter. His tongue stuck to the roof of his mouth as he attempted to force a raspy word from his dry throat. He stared at Kenny when his eyelids strengthened enough to stay open. Tonya handed Kenny a cup of water with a straw after he slowly raised the head of the electric hospital bed a few degrees to safely swallow.

"Am...I dead?"

"Fortunately, you are not." He replied as he gave him another sip of water.

"Good. I was thinking...that angels were...ugly."

"It is great to see that you haven't lost your sense of humor, Phillip."

"Pain..."

"I will get you something for that. Get some rest my friend. We'll talk soon."

Kenny administered medication into Phillips I.V. that lightly sedated him. He drifted off and appeared comfortable as Kenny checked his vitals, heart, and lung sounds. He looked over at Tonya and they both felt a wave of relief as this was a sign of hopefulness for all of them. He knew that it was time to initiate the next step in their plan.

CHAPTER SEVENTEEN

Renee used the elevator to descend 3 levels to answer the door. She used the intercom to alert Detective Twyman and Sneed that she would be there momentarily to receive their unannounced visit. Her heart raced as she simultaneously hoped and not hoped it was pertaining to Phillip.

She opened the door quickly and examined both of their faces as she asked if they had located Phillip without even inviting them in. She took a few deep breaths and invited them in.

"Excuse me if I am not a gracious host, detective. But I am certain that you didn't stop by for coffee."

"Sorry for the inconvenience, Mrs. Mathews. We just had a few more questions and hoped that you may have some knowledge that could help our investigation. Judging by your reaction, I take it that you haven't heard from your husband since we spoke last?" asked Detective Twyman as his partner observed in the background. Renee extended her hand inviting them to sit on the sofa in front of the window and she sat across from them in a chair anchoring the fireplace.

"No. I haven't heard from him."

"Can you tell us again about the last time the two of you spoke."

"Three weeks ago, Phillip took a trip to Italy to meet with someone or a new distributor to tour their olive grove. I would have gone but the International travel restrictions for expectant mother's prevented me from accompanying him. My best friend was flying to LA out of Logan, so I dropped her off and waited an hour for the flight from Fiumicino. He didn't get off the plane. The flight attendant said that all passengers had debarked."

"You told us that you called him from your cellphone a few times before leaving the airport, correct?" Detective Twyman asked while looking down at his notes.

"Correct. It went straight to voicemail each time before I left the airport and each time since."

"You also said that the two of you were not having marital problems, but you hadn't spoken in a week, and it was almost 2 weeks before he was reported as missing. Is that normal for the two of you to not have contact that long…especially since you are expecting a baby?"

Renee stood up holding her baby bump. She was annoyed and agitated by their line of questions. In hindsight, she was embarrassed from the way she handled the entire situation. Before she could speak, she heard the key turn and the front door open. Denise walked in carrying packages and announced that she was going to run upstairs and change her clothes so that they could leave for Lamaze class in 30 minutes. She noticed as she entered further into the house the presence of the 2 detectives sitting on the sofa in front of where Renee was standing. They both stood up when they saw Denise. She placed her packages on the round table in the foyer and joined Renee and the detectives in the living room.

"Madam ADA," led Detective Sneed.

"Detectives," she replied. then looked at Renee who clearly looked uncomfortable. She moved closer to comfort her, then faced the detectives with an analyzing look.

"We are here following up on some information we gathered

from Mrs. Mathews that may help with our investigation."

"Do you have any leads?"

The detectives looked at one another then Detective Sneed spoke.

"The management of the villa in Italy said that the American that rented the property left yesterday. They could not confirm that it was Phillip Mathews because he opted for self-check-in and check-out and did not need any assistance during his stay. They could not confirm how many guests, no disrespect Mrs. Mathews. So, it appears like he is not missing."

"That makes absolutely no sense at all! Phillip would never, ever, not communicate with me. He would never do that!" Denise instructed Renee to calm down.

"Are you sure this Villa keeper is legit, or the information is reliable?" Denise asked.

"Well, we can't be 100% sure. We have not found the name of the individual he flew there to meet or which olive grove he was to visit. Oddly, none of Mathews' staff at the Wooden Spoon had any information on the vendor he was meeting with. Our resources are limited when it comes to international investigations. There are so many types of police in Italy. I did speak with a Corporal Razo who said that he would look into it and get back with me," replied Detective Twyman. "Did you know that everyone closes up for lunch and takes a nap?" Twyman saw that no one in the room except for his partner finds this revelation interesting; he stood and prepared himself to end their meeting.

"We see that you have an appointment, so I wanted to ask you before we leave if you are aware that your husband was seeing a therapist?"

"Yes, I am. I suggested that he speak to someone professionally after his father's trial."

"Would you happen to know the therapist's name? Maybe he could share some insight on his state of mind."

"I think it is Bailey, Dr. Nicolas Bailey. His office is on Staniford Street, if I'm not mistaken."

"Interesting. Thank you, ma'am. If you do hear from your husband, please give us a call. If we find anything, we will give you a call," concluded Detective Twyman.

The detectives walked to the door after shaking hands with Renee and Denise. Renee did not show them out, but she stopped them and called out to them from where she stood.

"Detectives, please find my husband. Each day that passes, I get more worried that you or someone else will ring the doorbell with bad news."

"We will do our best, Mrs. Mathews," assured Twyman.

CHAPTER EIGHTEEN

The same news story flooded the internet and hit every television station across the airways like a catastrophic tornado without a warning. Renee, Denise, Calvin, and Russell gathered in front of the television and tuned in like most Americans were today with their morning coffee as arrests staggered across the state in an alarming magnitude.

Viewers watched handcuffed business owners and elected officials be placed in the back of the white and blue squad cars. The country saw several computers and boxes being placed by federal law enforcement into the back of black utility vehicles. The list of individuals who were still at large to be taken into custody or questioned read more like a guest list for a political fundraiser event than a sting arrest list.

It was no surprise to Renee that newscaster, Brenda Ray who hosts Boston's news show, *The HUB,* was in full on journalist mode considering the headline stories of the day. Renee rolled her eyes and sighed quickly as Brenda Ray spoke before the cameras into her microphone, as if her single successful interview a few years ago with Renee, combined with her unsuccessful romantic past with Phillip implied that she was connected to the Mathews inner family circle.

"Yes David, we have been camped out in front of New England's Level 1 Trauma Center in Rhode Island since the break of dawn. As one would have it, the mystery surrounding the disappearance of Celebrity Chef and Restaurateur, Phillip Mathews, Jr. is superseded and overshadowed by the insurmountable and inscrutable trail leading to his reemergence.

We have not been able to see Mr. Mathews due to the volume of security led by federal agents. Access to some of the hospital floors are blocked off. The hospital will not give out any information to the public at this time.

A spokesperson for the Mathews family has declined any comment at this time on his condition or the family's reaction to the apparent suicide death of Phillip Mathews Sr. from his prison cell at the Federal Medical Center in Devens. He was serving a 25 year sentence for the attempted murder of one said Russell Mark Cambridge, II, his friend and business partner. Phillip Mathews Sr. was said to have been awaiting future trials for charges linked to several organized crime.

We will keep you posted with any new developments. This is Brenda Ray reporting live from Providence, Rhode Island. Now back to you David."

Renee exhaled a sigh of relief as Denise turned the channel with the remote control and adjusted the volume to low. Attention suddenly turned as the hospital room door opened. Detectives Sneed and Twyman entered the room after being granted access by the two armed guards standing in the hallway at the door.

"Mrs. Mathews. ADA Ruckus-Jacobs," respectfully greeted Detective Twyman. "We were wondering how Mr. Mathews was doing and if he was up for answering questions."

Renee kissed Phillip on the forehead and excused herself after handing him a sip of water from the straw placed in the water pitcher on the bedside table. She reminded him that the doctor instructed him not to exhaust himself. Calvin and Russell escorted her to the staff lounge where they were given permission to utilize for coffee, meals, or to stretch their legs away from the media. Renee felt comforted knowing that Denise would be present at the bedside to ensure that her husband's well-being was a priority.

"Mr. Mathews. My name is Detective Marvin Twyman, and this is my partner Detective Sneed. We responded to an anonymous tip and ended up here when the ambulance brought you here last night. Can you tell us where you have been for the past month and how you ended up on a boat at the Yacht Club in Edgewood?"

"I already made a statement to the FBI Agents earlier. I don't know if I can shed any more light on anything. It's all still blurry to me."

"Yes. I understand and I have read over your statement, but we might be able to pick up on some details that those guys missed."

"Like I said, I got a call from my therapist the morning of my trip to Italy. He said that he had a cancellation and could squeeze me in. He had been seriously helping me through this crazy insomnia.

I had been having some major trouble sleeping. He does this relaxation technique that keeps me from taking pills."

"Did you and your therapist ever have any personal or business connections besides these relaxation treatments?" asked Detective Sneed.

"Outside of our therapy sessions, we had engaged in a few conversations about him selling his boat. I hinted that I may be an interested buyer. I mentioned that I was considering making the purchase before the baby comes. It turned out that we both had a few hours to kill, so we decided to kill 2 birds with one stone and have our session on his yacht. That way, I could check it out. The last thing that I can remember is meeting him outside of his office and riding with him to the Marina on the Bay. At least that is what I think happened. Everything after that and some of the before is a blank or fuzzy in my brain."

Renee returned to Phillip's hospital room alone with a cup of coffee in hand. She handed the coffee to Denise, then walked over to the opposite side of the bed where the detectives stood. She lovingly reached for her husband's hand and smiled down at him.

"Detectives. I think that we should let the patient rest now. Can we step outside for a moment?" Denise asked. The detectives said goodbye to the Mathews couple and followed the Assistant District Attorney out of the room and into the hallway.

"So gentlemen, the pharmacology reports showed that Phillip had an excessive amounts of sedatives in his system. The physician attributes that this is why there are gaps in his memory. He also said that he may or may not get more memories back over a few weeks. Lastly, he appears to have had some type of surgical procedure performed on him to which he has no recollection. From the look of all the copies of videos dropped at every news station and publication, and it looks as if he may have been a victim of an elaborate organ harvesting ring."

"Yeah, there's a lot of job openings today," Sneed smirked. "And it ain't just top officials either. The Blue Lasso rounded up two Pop-up Human Chop-shops. Connecting all of these cases, including these back alley clinics run by med-school drop-outs and the internet taught surgeons performing illegal abortions, bargain price plastic surgery, and God knows what else will be an undertaking."

"I agree, there's certainly a connection. We do know that Dr. Bailey used concealed devices to videotape all of his sessions in his office and at the prison. He even taped his meetings. But the money question is; if he was found dead of a heart attack weeks ago, then who was it that sent all of the video tapes last night?" replied Twyman.

"I take it that the warden has not been located yet?" Denise inquired.

"Nope. That is no big surprise, but I still can't believe for the life of me that Mathews Senior hung himself," adds Sneed.

"Found hung partner... and if I may speak ill of the dead, I don't think monsters commit suicide," countered Detective Twyman. "Oh by the way, we spoke to the paramedics last night and listened to the 911 call from the marina security guard."

"Did you happen to get anything?"

"Just more questions. We're going to head over to the Marina now and take a look around the boat before going back to the city. I heard that the coast guard confiscated two floating operating room yachts. Crazy turn of events, huh? But I'm sure we'll talk soon, Madam ADA."

CHAPTER NINETEEN

Denise left the hospital but not before she whispered in Renee ear a code phrase, *control/alt/delete*. From that moment on, it was understood that she was not to ever discuss anything that transpired this week again. Not at home with Phillip. Not with anyone. Not anywhere. The honor among thieves and criminal street justice prevailed with the delivery of all players who were sacrificed to ensure the safety of Phillip, his family, and whoever aided him through this ordeal. Denise's involvement and actions moving forward was to secure convictions.

Phillip shut his eyes and drifted deep in thought before closing the chapters on the memories that would never come light. He bid a mental farewell to being warned by the Bailey brothers that he was being watched by his father and perhaps powerful persons a part of an organization that was involved in trafficking organs and narcotics.

His second hand knowledge that illicit drugs were being surgically implanted in animal or human cadavers, or inside of living human serving as mules to transport in or out of the country had to vanish.

He figuratively had to hit a delete button regarding the mention of countless patients consenting to a specific surgical procedure, only to unknowingly have an organ harvested.

Phillip took longer to close the box on the fact that much of the corruption exposure planning was used under pretense as their therapy sessions. He assumed that things must have gone critically wrong somehow, that he ended up on an operating table and that Nick Baily was dead; since neither of the scenarios were a part of the plan to take down part of an organization.

They both knew that the doctor was in too deep to escape fully unscathed. Dr. Baily admitted to Phillip that he was aware that even providing the organization with patient information related to their personal demographics, health questionnaire results, marital status, address, and daily routines were not no harm crimes.   But even as his therapist's actions began to eat away at him, circumstances of one thing or another like debt or protecting his brother, just pulled him deeper into sinister involvement.

Phillip just heard one of the news reporters mention that based on the contents of the videotapes of Dr. Nicholas Bailey, an autopsy was to be done to rule out foul play on what was presumed a heart attack in a reasonably healthy man.

Phillip gave the final goodbye thought to that of the ledger that Russell found. It was hidden and belonged to Senior. It contained the names of government officials who were involved in many dealings and details that if in the right or wrong hands would cause detriment to nations and individuals. The ledger served as a bargaining chip as good faith to include the cost of safe passage for a new life for Kenny and Tonya once it was given to a foreign leader with the power to protect and to destroy. Phillip could never think again about the knowledge that his friend Russell passed the ledger to Octavia who traveled without suspicion to place the ledger in the Villa in Italy for retrieval by the lesser of evils that would guarantee the fate of their futures.

The last thought that delivering the ledger also served Senior on a platter, as clearly it showed that he would have double crossed one, some, or all when the opportunity presented itself. Phillip still found it difficult to believe that not only did Senior steal his kidney but knowing that his father's instructions were that he was to be left on the operating table to die hurt him in a place he thought was numb. He just inhaled deeply and let go of the thought. He was able to file it away in the discard pile in his mind labelled, forgettable. It sat right behind the pile with visions of the media being up in a frenzy over who else was to be rounded up for arrest by the FBI and DEA agencies.

The fact of the matter was that Phillip had no knowledge of who was considered to be expendable. He was to just made sure that burner phones were sent to Renee, Russell, and Denise a week ago in order to get security to call paramedics, and to get officers from both local law enforcement and the FBI to be present to receive him in a sedated state.

Renee sat in a reclining chair next to Phillip's hospital bed. She drifted to sleep thinking of the last pages that she read in the tin box written by Elizabeth.

◆ ◆ ◆

As I trained my replacement and the new generation of Manor-keepers, I began to fade into the floral wallpaper once young Phillip had become the master of the estate. Unforgiven, I was invisible to him since the day at the cemetery. I sincerely cared for the boy almost half my age, that I protected and watched grow from a lonely, troubled child to a dark, troubled man.

I had once hoped that his beautiful and innocent bride, Rose Marie, could shine a light upon him that could brighten his black heart and lost soul, but as a secret keeper, I turned a blind eye to the fact that her fate eventually mimicked Phillip's infant brother, Elliot, and by the same hands.

Luckily, Phillip's son, who bore his name, did not inherit the same evil in his eyes. The light that Rose Marie could not shine on her husband, was abundantly radiant within her son whom she loved and was loved back by him, regardless of how much his father tried to mold him. I was a spectator in awe to see what parent-child love looked like.

❖ ❖ ❖

Soon after, anything that resembled happiness for me vanished when Ethan Lee left the earth. The news of his fatal accident sent the Manor into mourning.

It was unlike any time when a Mathews family member had passed away. This time, there was a genuine sense of sadness throughout as if the very walls themselves wept. Our secret walks, our conversations became fewer and less frequent once Sir Simon forbade staff fraternizing. I recall this rule being instituted the day after I stood outside of Sir Simon's study and eavesdropped as Ethan Lee formally requested permission to marry me.

I knew that Sir Simon had no use for me outside of my servant role, but I thought that his fondness for Ethan Lee, his most loyal staff, would warrant granting one request. I was wrong. I assumed and even secretly hoped that one day Sir Simon would depart this life before Ethan Lee and myself, leaving us to love freely. I was wrong.

My Ethan fell victim to the 5th Season. The time of year when winter and spring clash for dominance. That window of time when the earth's soil is too wet to yield life, but the mud swallows' life. The blisters of winter push hard to remain in power longer than entitled, while the power of seeds hope to flourish sooner than expected.

Hope inevitably has casualties. My hope was delivered and turned out to be a tin box with secrets now wrapped with a scarlet red ribbon.

CHAPTER TWENTY

Renee leaned back in Phillip's arm cradling their beautiful daughter. They counted ten toes and tenfingers. They marveled at how alert and wide-eyed she was to be only hours old.

"She is so beautiful, Phillip."

"She is beautiful. Just like her mother. I promise to love and cherish both of my girls forever. I will do right by her and protect her."

"I know you will, baby."

"Hey, have we decided on a name? We agreed that if our baby was a boy, I would pick his name. If we had a girl, then you had the honor. Remember?"

"Yes. I remember," she giggled lightly.

"And?"

"And...I was thinking of Elizabeth-Rose. One hyphenated first name. Too much?"

"No. I don't think it's too much at all. I think that Elizabeth to honor your mother, and Rose to honor mine is thoughtful and sweet. I love it."

"Well Babe, you are right about honoring your mother, but there are two Elizabeth's that I would like to honor. One is my mother, yes. And the other...well the other is your Great-Aunt Elizabeth," Renee stumbled to get the words out of her brain, off of her tongue, and into the open air.

"Great-Aunt? Honey, I don't have an aunt or a great aunt," Phillip chuckled.

"True, you don't have one now, but you did once upon a time. She deserved to be acknowledged in her lifetime, but unfortunately she wasn't. She was hidden. Until now.

Let me tell you a story..."

The End

ABOUT THE AUTHOR

E. G. Fahie

Credited with writing 4 successful gospel stage play productions, this faith-based writer, 2-time Novella author, and freelance literary editor is a Washington, D.C. native who discovered her love for writing in college while studying to become a Registered Nurse.

She prides herself on being multi-talented and the wearer of many hats, as she combines the love of her craft with her successful medical career in several writing rooms as a writer, co-writer, set designer, executive producer, and story consultant with renown Los Angeles based multimedia production company, TB MEDIA. Her creativity and entrepreneurship is celebrated on and off the red carpet with her event planning and set-design company.

Proclaiming that wife, mother, and grandmother are her favorite titles, she understands the meaning of true dedication, which translates across the pages of her work, and welcomes the reader into the lives of her characters.

BOOKS BY THIS AUTHOR

After The Mud Season

Maintaining relationships prove to be challenging for a group of late iGen professionals attempting to carve their mark in Boston's prominent social and business community.

When circumstances and outside forces prove their inability to withstand the complexity of ego and heartbreak, the beautiful and brilliant tech savvy, Renee Brown and former playboy and restaurateur, Phillip Mathews are forced to end their engagement and an 8-year relationship.

The legal battle that follows this power couple's break-up is brutal. The scars from social media and tabloid justice run deep leaving a trail of casualties and unhealed wounds, forcing their close-knit circle of friends to choose sides of loyalty, ultimately forging an unlikely alliance to neutralize a common enemy.

ACKNOWLEDGEMENT

To my CH Roommates:

Regardless of where we are, where we have been, or we are going in life, we choose each other.
Thank you for showing up for you, and for showing up for me.
We continue to selflessly encourage one another no matter what is going on in our lives.
Your support and the vibe when we are together creates a magical energy that I will be forever grateful for.
Keep winning and count on me to be cheering for you every step of the way.

www.ingramcontent.com/pod-product-compliance
Lightning Source LLC
Chambersburg PA
CBHW060743180626
46819CB00001B/73